# Betsy's Play School

*Published by Harcourt Brace Jovanovich, Inc.*

# By the Same Author

*Published by William Morrow & Company*

A VALENTINE FANTASY. 1976
EDDIE'S VALUABLE PROPERTY. 1975
"C" IS FOR CUPCAKE. 1974
AWAY WENT THE BALLOONS. 1973
A CHRISTMAS FANTASY. 1972
EDDIE'S HAPPENINGS. 1971
MERRY CHRISTMAS FROM BETSY. 1970
TAFFY AND MELISSA MOLASSES. 1969
EVER-READY EDDIE. 1968
BETSY AND MR. KILPATRICK. 1967
EDDIE THE DOG HOLDER. 1966
ROBERT ROWS THE RIVER. 1965
EDDIE'S GREEN THUMB. 1964
HERE COMES THE BUS! 1963
SNOWBOUND WITH BETSY. 1962
ANNIE PAT AND EDDIE. 1960
EDDIE AND LOUELLA. 1959
BETSY'S WINTERHOUSE. 1958
EDDIE MAKES MUSIC. 1957
BETSY'S BUSY SUMMER. 1956
EDDIE AND HIS BIG DEALS. 1955
BETSY AND THE CIRCUS. 1954
EDDIE'S PAY DIRT. 1953
THE MIXED-UP TWINS. 1952
EDDIE AND GARDENIA. 1951
BETSY'S LITTLE STAR. 1950
EDDIE AND THE FIRE ENGINE. 1949
PENNY GOES TO CAMP. 1948
LITTLE EDDIE. 1947

# Betsy's Play School

## CAROLYN HAYWOOD

illustrated by James Griffin

William Morrow and Company

New York 1977

Library of Congress Cataloging in Publication Data

Haywood, Carolyn (date)
    Betsy's play school.

    SUMMARY: Betsy organizes a summer play school for six neighbor-hood children.
    [1. Play schools—Fiction]    I. Griffin, James, 1949-    II. Title.
PZ7.H31496Bn      [Fic]        77-1615
ISBN 0-688-22115-7
ISBN 0-688-32115-1 lib. bdg.

cc,series  7/6/10 MPK

Dedicated with love

to

Lynn and Anne Boynton

# CONTENTS

# Betsy's Play School

# Chapter 1

# BETSY HAS AN IDEA

SCHOOL HAD CLOSED for the summer vacation. Many of the children were finding ways to earn some money of their own. One day Betsy said to her mother, "Ellen's brother is going to make a lot of money during the summer."

"How is he going to make a lot of money?" her mother asked.

"He's going to help weed gardens," said Betsy, "and everyone he helps is going to pay him."

"That's a very good way to earn a little money during the summer," said Betsy's mother.

"I've been thinking," said Betsy, "I'd like to earn some money too, and I have an idea."

"Tell me about it," said her mother.

"I'd like to have a play school," said Betsy. "I bet a lot of mothers would be glad to send their children to my school in the mornings."

"Where are you planning to hold this play school?" her mother asked.

"Oh, in our basement playroom," Betsy replied.

"But Betsy," said her mother, "some mothers may feel that you're still too young to look after their little ones."

"You don't think so, do you, Mother?" Betsy asked.

Betsy's mother looked at her lovingly. "I think you're very responsible. You've always taken good care of your little sister Star."

"Star could come to my school whenever she wanted to," said Betsy. "And her friend Lilly-bell too. She almost lives here, because she comes every day to play with Star. They could come to my play school for nothing."

"You mean you would give them scholarships?" her mother asked.

Betsy laughed. "Yes, they would be free pupils with scholarships."

"It sounds like a real school now," said her mother. "How much are you going to charge?"

"Would fifty cents a morning for each child be all right?" Betsy asked.

"Yes, I think so," said her mother.

"There are a lot of little children around here," said Betsy. "Those people who have moved into the house on the corner of our street have a little girl. Her name is Rosalie Bottom, but they call her Rosie."

"Rosie Bottom!" her mother exclaimed. "What an unusual name!"

Betsy laughed. "If they had named her Bell, then she would be called Bell Bottom, wouldn't she?"

"Yes," her mother agreed, laughing. "Or Buster Bottom if she'd been a boy."

Now Betsy and her mother were both giggling. Finally Betsy said, "There are the Cooley twins, too. I'll bet Mrs. Cooley would send the twins to my school."

"Oh, Betsy!" exclaimed her mother, "You couldn't have the Cooley twins. They're still in diapers."

"How do you know?" Betsy asked.

"I know because they waddle like two little ducks," her mother replied, "and you couldn't change their diapers."

"Oh, yes, I could," said Betsy.

"No diapers!" said her mother very firmly.

"Well, I'll bet I could get little Fay Foster," said Betsy. "She must be out of diapers. I think I'll go over right now and ask Mrs. Foster if Fay can come to my school."

Betsy ran off down the street. When she reached the corner, Rodney West appeared on his tricycle. "Hello, Rodney!" said Betsy. "Would you like to come to my play school? It's going to be fun with a lot of children. I'm going to have it in our basement playroom."

"Can I bring Bobo?" Rodney asked.

"Who's Bobo?" asked Betsy.

"He's my friend," Rodney replied.

"Of course you can bring Bobo," said Betsy.

"Can he bring his dog?" Rodney wanted to know next.

"Oh, no!" exclaimed Betsy. "We can't have dogs in school."

"Oh!" said Rodney. "Well, I'd like to come anyway."

"I'll talk to your mother," said Betsy.

"She isn't home now," said Rodney.

"Then I'll talk to her another time," said Betsy. "Good-bye, Rodney."

" 'Bye!" Rodney replied and pedaled off.

Betsy went on to Fay's house. When she arrived she found that Fay was having a birthday party.

"Oh, Betsy!" said Mrs. Foster, as she opened the door. "I'm sorry there isn't room for you at the table but do come in."

Betsy walked into the room. Seven children were gathered around the table, and Fay was seated at the end. Mrs. Foster didn't seem busy at that moment, so Betsy told her about her plan to have a play school during the summer. "I thought perhaps you would like to send Fay," said Betsy.

"Oh, Betsy!" said Mrs. Foster. "You're much too young to take charge of little children. I couldn't leave Fay with you for a whole morning."

Betsy looked sad. "Mother thinks I could take care of them." she said.

"I'm afraid I don't agree with your mother," said Mrs. Foster.

Just then Fay called out, "Mommy, where's the cake?"

"Excuse me, Betsy," said Mrs. Foster. "I have to get the birthday cake."

Mrs. Foster went into the kitchen. When she came back she was carrying the birthday cake with four lighted candles in one hand and a pitcher of lemonade in the other. Mrs. Foster placed the cake in front of Fay whose face was shining with happiness at having such a beautiful birthday cake.

Betsy looked at Fay's blue eyes and her fine,

silky golden hair that hung down on each side of her face. What a pretty little girl she is, Betsy thought.

"Blow, Fay, blow!" the children began to call out.

Fay puckered up her lips and prepared to blow out the candles. She leaned over the cake. As she did so, her hair fell forward. In an instant the flame from the lighted candles caught the ends of Fay's hair and Fay's hair was on fire.

Mrs. Foster screamed, but Betsy, who was nearer the table, picked up the pitcher of lemonade and poured it over Fay's head. Fay started screaming, but her hair was no longer on fire.

Mrs. Foster rushed to Fay and threw her arms around her. As soon as she knew that Fay was all right she turned to Betsy. "Oh, Betsy!" she said. "How quick you were! You saved Fay's life."

Fay was crying. "Betsy spoiled my birthday cake," she said, sobbing. "It's all wet, and she

put the candles out. She didn't let me blow them out."

"Why, Fay!" said her mother. "Don't cry about the cake. Your hair was on fire, and Betsy kept you from being badly burned."

Then Mrs. Foster said to Betsy, "I was wrong to think you couldn't take care of little children. I'll be happy to put Fay in your play school. Now do have some ice cream with the children."

Betsy was delighted. "Thank you, Mrs. Foster," she said, "but I want to see Rodney's mother." Perhaps she could find more pupils that afternoon.

Rodney was still on his tricycle when Betsy reached his house. "Mommy isn't home yet," said Rodney. Then he added, "Bobo doesn't want to come to your school."

"I'm sorry," said Betsy. "Why doesn't he want to come?"

" 'Cause he can't bring his dog Tinkie," Rodney answered.

"Where is Bobo?" Betsy asked Rodney.

"I spanked Tinkie, and Bobo took him into the house," said Rodney.

"Why did you spank Tinkie?" Betsy asked.

"Because he bit the mailman," Rodney replied.

"Oh," cried Betsy, "the poor mailman!"

"He bit the mailman on the leg," said Rodney, "and he tore his pants. The ambulance came and took him to the hospital."

"Bobo shouldn't have such a vicious dog," said Betsy. "I don't want a vicious dog like that in my school."

When Betsy reached home, she said to her mother, "I may have two children for my school already. I have Fay for sure, and I think Rodney West will come too."

"How nice," her mother replied.

A short time later the doorbell rang, and Betsy went to the door. When she opened it she was surprised to see the mailman. "Why, Mr. Carter!" she exclaimed. "Are you all right? I'm glad you didn't have to stay in the hospital."

"Hospital!" exclaimed Mr. Carter. "I haven't been in the hospital."

"Rodney West said his friend Bobo's dog bit you in the leg."

Mr. Carter threw back his head and laughed. "Oh, that Rodney," he said. "It's all make-believe. His friend Bobo is make-believe and so is the dog. Rodney had a make-believe horse once, and he used to tell me about the horse. It won races and made a lot of money for Rodney's dad. Then one day it broke its leg, and they had to shoot it. You should have been with me the morning Rodney told me that story. I thought he was going to cry real tears over that make-believe horse. That kid needs some real friends and a

real dog. I don't know where they would keep
a real horse, though."

Betsy laughed. "He'll have some real friends
soon if his mother lets him come to my summer
school. I'll tell him he can bring his friend Bobo
and the dog too."

*Chapter 2*

# BETSY GETS
# SOME MORE PUPILS

BETSY TALKED a great deal about her plans for her summer school. In fact, she talked about it all the time. "I'll tell them a story every day," she said, "and I'm going to take them for a walk every day. We'll play games in the yard, and I'll take them to the zoo."

"Not alone," said her mother.

"Oh, no!" exclaimed Betsy. "You'll go with me."

"So I'm to be a helper in this school?" her mother questioned. "How much do I get paid for helping?"

"Oh, hugs and kisses," said Betsy.

"Hugs and kisses!" her mother exclaimed, laughing. "That won't buy the groceries."

"But Daddy pays for the groceries," Betsy said, joining her mother's laughter.

"Very well," said her mother. "I can see I'm going to the zoo."

"You'll have fun, Mommy," said Betsy.

Just then Betsy's little sister, Star, came in with her best friend, Lillybell.

"Hello, Lillybell!" said Betsy. "Did you know that I'm going to have a play school for the children who live nearby?"

"Star told me," Lillybell replied. "My little cousin Sammy just moved near here. Maybe he would like to come to your school."

"Where does Sammy live?" Betsy asked.

"Just over on North Street," Lillybell replied. "His daddy keeps chickens. They never have to buy any eggs, 'cause the chickens lay the eggs for them."

"Oh, fresh eggs," said Betsy.

"Sammy has a pet chicken," said Lillybell. "It's a white chicken, and it follows him all around. It's just like Mary's little lamb."

Betsy and Star laughed. Then Betsy said, "I hope it won't follow him to school one day."

"I guess it will," said Lillybell. "Sammy's just crazy about that chicken."

The following day Betsy went to see Sammy's mother to tell her about the school. Sammy's mother called him in from the backyard. He came in carrying a white chicken. "Sammy!" his mother said. "Put that chicken down, and shake hands with Lillybell's friend Betsy. You're going to go to her play school. You'll like that. You can play with a lot of little kids."

"I can't shake hands," said Sammy, "'cause I have to hold Mona."

"Put that chicken down," said his mother, "and shake hands properly."

Sammy put the chicken down in Betsy's lap. "You hold Mona," he said, "so I can shake hands."

"Oh, oh!" cried Betsy. "She won't lay an egg in my lap, will she?"

Shaking Betsy's hand, Sammy said, "She only lays eggs in her nest. Can I bring Mona to school?"

"Someday you can bring her," said Betsy, "to

show to the children. But you can't bring her every day."

"OK," said Sammy. "She's a very friendly chicken, and I love her very much." He took up his chicken and smoothed her head and back. "She's pretty, isn't she?" he asked Betsy.

"She's very pretty," Betsy replied.

"I raised her from a baby chick," said Sammy. "I guess she thinks I'm her daddy."

Sammy's mother interrupted. "He'll talk about that chicken the rest of the day," she said. "Are you thinking of getting Jackie Oakie for your school, Betsy?"

"I don't know Jackie Oakie," said Betsy. "Where does he live?"

"Right up the street, just two doors away," said Sammy's mother. "Only Jackie's a girl, not a boy."

"Oh," said Betsy. "Do you think I could go now to see Jackie's mother?"

"Sure, why not?" Sammy's mother replied. "You tell her Sammy's mother, Mrs. Rupie, sent you."

Betsy got up. "I'll go right away," she said. "My play school starts on Monday."

"Sammy will be there," said his mother.

Betsy ran up the street to Jackie's house. When she pressed the bell, a loud barking started inside. "Oh," said Betsy, "I hope that's a friendly dog!"

In a few moments a smiling woman opened the door. A little girl stood behind her. "Hello!" she said to Betsy. "What can I do for you?"

"I'm Betsy," said Betsy, raising her voice above the dog's barking, "and I'm starting a summer school for little kids. Mrs. Rupie said I should ask if Jackie could come to my school. She's sending Sammy."

Mrs. Oakie shouted at the dog. "Be quiet, Toby!" But Toby ran forward and jumped on Betsy, who drew back. "He won't hurt you,"

said Mrs. Oakie. "He just hasn't any manners, but he's going to school. Obedience School they call it. I sure hope he learns to behave himself."

Jackie spoke up. "He goes to school to learn to be a good dog, and he's going to graduate. Do you know what *graduate* means?"

"Yes," replied Betsy. "It means that he does everything he's told to do."

Toby kept right on jumping on Betsy, and Mrs. Oakie kept right on saying, "Down, Toby, down!" In between barks she told Betsy that she would be glad to put Jackie in the summer school.

Betsy felt that Toby hadn't learned very much about obedience so far. She wondered whether he would graduate.

When Betsy left she walked to the house of her friend, Billy Porter. The Porters had adopted a little girl, so Billy now had a sister. Her name was Nancy.

Billy was wheeling his bicycle up the driveway when Betsy arrived. "Hi, Betsy!" Billy called out, when he saw her.

"Hi, Billy!" Betsy replied. "Did you hear I'm going to have a summer school?"

"How come?" said Billy. "What do you want to do that for?"

"To make some money," Betsy replied.

"What are you going to do with it?" Billy asked.

"Oh, lots of things," said Betsy. "Maybe I'll buy you a Christmas present with some of it!"

"Great!" Billy replied. "I hope you make a lot and buy me a pony."

Betsy laughed. "I came to see if your mother will send Nancy to my school."

"Oh, that way my mother will help to buy my Christmas present," said Billy. "You're a smart one, Betsy."

Betsy laughed. "I'll tell Santa Claus you want a pony."

"I've been telling him for years," said Billy. "I don't think he reads his mail."

"Where's your mother?" Betsy asked.

"In the kitchen," Billy replied. "Go 'round the back."

Betsy went to the kitchen door and knocked.

Mrs. Porter opened the door. "Why, Betsy!" she said. "How nice to see you. Come in."

Betsy stepped into the kitchen. In a few minutes she told Mrs. Porter about her school, and Mrs. Porter said that she thought it was a fine idea and that she would send Nancy.

Now Betsy had five pupils, and she wanted only one more. On her way home she decided to call on Mrs. Bottom to see if she would send her little girl to the school.

When Betsy reached the house on the corner,

she found a young girl sweeping the front steps. "Good morning!" said Betsy. "Are you Mrs. Bottom?"

"No, I'm Maggie," the girl replied. "I work for Mrs. Bottom, and I look after her children. There are three of them. Percy he's nine, and Buster he's two. Then Rosalie she's four. She's the middle one. I call them Big Bottom, Little Bottom, and Rosie Bottom."

"Is Mrs. Bottom at home?" Betsy asked.

"Yes, she's upstairs," Maggie replied. "You want to see her?"

"Yes, please," said Betsy.

Maggie led the way into the house, talking all the time. "Most of the time they're good kids, but sometimes they don't mind what I say. Then I just give them a slap on their you-know-what."

Betsy laughed. "I'm sure you don't hurt them," she said.

"Oh, no," said Maggie, "but it works. I'll tell Mrs. Bottom you want to see her," and she rushed upstairs.

When Mrs. Bottom came down, Betsy told her of her plans. Mrs. Bottom asked how long Rosalie would be at school, and Betsy replied, "From nine to twelve. They'll have milk and cookies at ten thirty and a half-hour rest if they bring sleeping bags."

"I think it's a lovely idea," said Mrs. Bottom. "I'll be delighted to send Rosalie."

When Betsy reached home she told her mother she now had six children for her school. In the evening Betsy told her father the news, too. Then she said, "Daddy, I have to have a place to keep the milk for the children."

"The milk!" her father exclaimed. "I suppose you want me to buy a cow."

"Oh, no, not a cow," said Betsy. "Just a nice little refrigerator to put downstairs in the play-room."

"A refrigerator?" her father repeated. "A refrigerator costs about as much as a cow."

"Just a little refrigerator," said Betsy. "I saw one in the window of the five and ten."

"Five and ten!" said her father, putting his hand in his pocket and pulling out a dime. "Here, Betsy, go buy yourself a refrigerator at the five and ten."

"Oh, Daddy," said Betsy. "Just because the refrigerator is in the window of the five and ten doesn't mean it's only ten cents. They sell more expensive things too."

"I knew this was a fishy story," said her father.

"Oh, Daddy," said Betsy, and they both laughed.

*Chapter 3*

# THE REFRIGERATOR

AT BREAKFAST on Saturday, Betsy's first re-
mark was, "Daddy, what about the refrigerator?"

"Oh, yes, the refrigerator," said her father.
"Are you sure you have to have a refrigerator?"

"I have to give the children milk and cookies,"
Betsy replied, "so I have to have a refrigerator."

45

"Refrigerators are very expensive," said her father, "even little ones. Are you sure the only way you can get a refrigerator is for me to buy one?"

"Well," said Betsy, "I could ask Eddie Wilson if he has one he could lend me. Eddie collects junk, and he might have one in his junk pile."

"Good idea," said her father. "See if Eddie has a junk refrigerator."

Betsy went to the telephone and called her friend Eddie. When he answered, she said, "Hi, Eddie! This is Betsy. Do you have a refrigerator in your junk pile?"

"You mean in my valuable property?" Eddie replied.

"Excuse me," said Betsy. "Of course I mean your valuable property."

"No," replied Eddie. "But I bet I could find one. Why do you need a refrigerator?"

Betsy explained to Eddie.

"Maybe I could find one on the town dump," Eddie replied. "A lot of valuable property gets thrown on the town dump. Why don't you get on your bike, and I'll meet you there."

"OK," said Betsy, "I'll be right over." Then she said to her father and mother, "I'm going over to the town dump to meet Eddie. He thinks maybe we can find a refrigerator there."

"Well, good luck to you," said her father.

Betsy got on her bicycle and was soon on her way. As she neared the dump she could see Eddie poking around in the rubbish.

When Eddie saw Betsy approaching, he ran to meet her. Waving his arms, he cried, "I found one!"

"Honest?" said Betsy, as she got off her bicycle.

"A nice little one," Eddie replied. "Come along and see it."

Betsy followed Eddie. They passed great piles

of rubbish, old mattresses, battered-up pots and pans, broken chairs and tables, even an iron bed with brass knobs.

"Oh, boy!" said Eddie. "Brass knobs!" He unscrewed the knobs and put them in his pocket, saying, "Really valuable property."

Betsy laughed. "Come on, where's the refrigerator?"

Eddie led the way to a little refrigerator. "It's a bit beat up," he said.

"Does the door open?" Betsy asked, after looking it over.

"I haven't tried it," Eddie replied. "I just found it."

"Well, see if it opens up," said Betsy.

Eddie took hold of the handle and opened the door. The children stooped down and looked inside. "Well, look at that!" Eddie said.

"What?" said Betsy.

"There in the corner," said Eddie, pointing into the refrigerator.

Betsy looked. "Why, it's a little mouse!" she exclaimed. "A dear little field mouse."

"He's a cutie," said Eddie. "Look at his big ears."

"He's trembling," said Betsy. "Poor little fellow. He's scared. The door must have been open, and he jumped in. Then somebody must have closed it."

Eddie put his hand in and picked up the mouse. "It's all right," he said, petting the little mouse.

"I'm going to keep him to show to the children," said Betsy.

"No!" said Eddie. *"I'm* going to keep him. I found him, so he's mine."

"He was in my refrigerator, so he's mine," said Betsy.

"What do you mean 'your refrigerator'? I haven't given it to you yet."

"Of course you've given it to me," said Betsy. "You found it for me."

"Sure," said Eddie, "but did I say, 'Here, Betsy, here's your refrigerator'?"

"Well, no," said Betsy.

"Then it was mine when I found it," said Eddie, "and anything inside is mine, so that makes the mouse mine." Eddie petted the mouse. "I'm going to call him Bertie."

"Can I borrow him sometime for the children?" Betsy asked.

"Sure you can borrow him, but don't forget, Bertie is mine," said Eddie. "I'm going to find a box to put him in." Eddie soon found a box.

"Now how are we going to get this refrigerator over to my house?" Betsy asked. "If it just had wheels, you could tow it along in back of your bike."

"Sure," said Eddie. "If horses had wings, horses could fly. The refrigerator doesn't have wheels, so it can't roll along."

Betsy and Eddie stood looking down at the refrigerator. "What about your express wagon?" Betsy asked.

"It's too big for my express wagon," Eddie replied.

Just then a car horn sounded. Betsy and Eddie looked toward the road. There they saw a red police car. "Hi there!" came a voice from inside the car.

"Oh," cried Betsy, "I think it's our friend Mr. Kilpatrick." Betsy ran to the car followed by Eddie. Sure enough it was Mr. Kilpatrick. "Hi, Mr. Kilpatrick!" Betsy cried.

"And sure," said Mr. Kilpatrick, "what would you and Eddie be up to on the dump?"

"Oh, we just found a dandy refrigerator for my school," Betsy replied.

"So you're playing school," said Mr. Kilpatrick.

"It's for the neighborhood children," Betsy replied, "and I have to have a refrigerator to keep the children's milk."

"Oh, sure, sure, the children's milk. And how are you going to transport that refrigerator?" Mr. Kilpatrick asked.

"That's the problem," said Betsy with a very long face.

"Well," said Mr. Kilpatrick, "there's many a time I've seen you with a face like that, and every time it means 'Pat to the rescue.'"

"Oh, would you really, Mr. Kilpatrick?" exclaimed Betsy with a bright face.

"Sure, if we all give a good heave-ho, I think we can get it into the trunk of my car," said Mr. Kilpatrick, stepping out of his car.

Before long Mr. Kilpatrick and Eddie had

moved the refrigerator to the edge of the road. Then Eddie helped Mr. Kilpatrick lift it into the trunk of his car.

"Sure we're not getting much heave-ho from Betsy," said Mr. Kilpatrick.

"I'm being grateful, Mr. Kilpatrick, that you came along to help us," said Betsy. "You always do."

"That's right," said Eddie.

"Ever since first grade," said Betsy, "when you used to take me across the street on my way to school."

"Come along now," said Mr. Kilpatrick. "Hop on your bicycles, and I'll meet you over at Betsy's."

Betsy and Eddie picked up their bikes, and Eddie put the box in his bike basket.

"What's in the box, Eddie?" Mr. Kilpatrick asked.

"A cute little field mouse," Eddie replied. "We found him in the refrigerator."

"Alive?" Mr. Kilpatrick questioned.

"Sure is," Eddie replied. "I love little field mice. I'm going to keep him as a pet."

"But Eddie's going to lend him to me to show the children," said Betsy.

"That's good," said Mr. Kilpatrick. "Always be generous with mice."

Eddie laughed. Then he and Betsy climbed on their bikes and pedaled as fast as they could over to Betsy's house while Mr. Kilpatrick drove his car.

Before long they all had arrived in front of Betsy's house. "There's a door in the back," said Betsy, "that goes right into the playroom."

Mr. Kilpatrick drove into the driveway to the back of the house. Together he and Eddie got the refrigerator out of the trunk of the car. Then they moved it into the playroom and stood it near the door. "See if it works," said Mr. Kilpatrick. "If I moved that thing over here from the dump and it doesn't work, I'll throw it out the window."

"Oh, Mr. Kilpatrick," cried Betsy. "I certainly hope it works."

Eddie picked up the cord and plugged it into a nearby socket. They all listened, and when the motor sounded they sighed with relief.

"It's OK," Eddie cried.

Then the children thanked Mr. Kilpatrick. They followed him to his car and waved as he drove away. "Now I have to wash out this refrigerator," said Betsy, "since it was a mouse's house."

Betsy went out and returned with a bucket of water, soap and sponge, a scrubbing brush, and a can of disinfectant. "This must be clean, or I can't put the children's milk inside," she said.

Betsy opened the door of the refrigerator again; then she let out a cry. "Oh, oh, there's a spider in there, Eddie!"

"Oh, what's a little spider?" said Eddie.

"Well, you can have the little spider," said Betsy. "You take the spider and I'll take the mouse, or I'll take the mouse and you take the spider."

"How's that again?" said Eddie.

Betsy repeated, "You take the spider and I'll take the mouse, or I'll take the mouse and you take the spider."

"You didn't let me choose!" cried Eddie. "You never said mouse to me once."

"Well, you seem to like the spider," said Betsy.

"You should keep the spider," said Eddie. "It will show the children how spiders spin webs. It's educational."

"I don't want an educated spider," said Betsy.

"I didn't say it was educated," said Eddie. "I said it was educational."

"Well, I don't want it, so please take it out of my refrigerator," said Betsy.

"But your kids are missing something," said Eddie.

Eddie picked up a piece of newspaper from the top of a pile of newspapers and reached into the refrigerator for the spider. He picked it up and went outside to dispose of it. "Poor little fellow," said Eddie, "just kicked out of his nice house."

Betsy scrubbed the inside of the refrigerator vigorously. When it was clean, she closed the door. "Now no more animals can get into my refrigerator," she said. Then, turning to Eddie, she continued. "It would be nice if I could have the mouse to show the children on Monday," she said.

"But tomorrow is Sunday, and I was planning to take Bertie to Sunday school," said Eddie.

"To Sunday school!" said Betsy. "What do you think he is? A church mouse?"

"I guess you think he's a dormouse, because you found him inside the door of your refrigerator," said Eddie.

"But you will leave him here for the children, won't you?" said Betsy.

"OK," said Eddie. "Be sure to feed him, though. I don't want Bertie to starve."

"He's the fattest mouse I've ever seen," said Betsy. "Look at his big tummy. But I won't let him starve."

"I'll tear up some newspaper and put it in the box, so he'll be comfortable," said Eddie. Eddie tore up bits of paper, which he placed in the box. Then he made holes in the lid, saying, "I don't want him to suffocate in this box."

"He'll be all right," said Betsy. "I'll give him

sunflower seeds. Daddy gives sunflower seeds to the birds. I'll bet Bertie will like them."

Soon Eddie departed, leaving the box on a table.

All day Sunday Betsy kept running down to the playroom to lift the lid and peep at Bertie. He seemed to be busy tearing up the bits of newspaper.

On Monday morning, before the children arrived, Betsy lifted the lid of Bertie's box. She found him lying in the midst of the paper scraps, and beside him were what Betsy thought were eight pink jelly beans. Betsy was puzzled. Where could the jelly beans have come from? she wondered.

Betsy ran upstairs to her mother. "Mother," she said, "did you put some pink jelly beans in Bertie's box?"

"Certainly not!" her mother replied. "I

haven't seen any jelly beans around since Easter."

"Well, there are eight pink jelly beans in Bertie's box. You come and see," said Betsy.

Betsy's mother followed Betsy down to the playroom. Betsy lifted the lid of the box, and her mother looked down at Bertie.

"See the jelly beans?" said Betsy.

Her mother touched one of them gently. "Why, Betsy," she said, "they aren't jelly beans. They are baby field mice. They must just have been born."

"Oh, Mother," cried Betsy. "Are you sure?"

"I'm sure," said her mother. "Don't touch them. If you do, the mother won't feed them."

"But, Mother, this mouse is named Bertie. How can Bertie be a mother?"

"This mother just has the wrong name," said Betsy's mother. "It had better be changed to Bertha or Alberta."

Betsy rushed upstairs to the telephone. She soon had Eddie on the line. "Eddie," she said, "the most exciting thing has happened! Your mouse Bertie has eight babies. Do you want to change his name to Bertha or Alberta?"

"Now we know why that mouse had such a fat tummy," said Eddie. "He—she—was full of babies. I'll be over soon to see them."

"But what do you want to call her?" said Betsy.

"Bertha," said Eddie.

## Chapter 4

## JUST BETSY

"Mother," said Betsy on Monday morning at breakfast, "now that I have a school I think the children should call me Miss Betsy."

"Oh, Betsy!" her mother exclaimed. "Don't you think that's expecting too much from the children?"

"But, Mother, every teacher is either Mrs. Somebody or Miss Somebody."

"When I was a little girl in school," said her mother, "I remember we called the first-grade teacher Teacher Helen and our second-grade teacher was Teacher Ruth."

"Oh, that's nice," said Betsy. "I'll be Teacher Betsy."

Betsy was so anxious to show the mouse and the babies to the children that she could hardly wait for the children to arrive. At last they appeared, and by nine o'clock the six children were seated at a long table. "Oh, children," said Betsy, "you'll never guess what I have to show you!" Betsy picked up the mouse's box, and the children left their chairs and gathered around Betsy.

"What is it? What is it?" they asked.

"You just wait and see," said Betsy, as she placed the box in front of her on the table. Then she lifted the lid.

Rosie Bottom cried out, "Oh! Oh! It's a mouse! I'm afraid of mice."

"Now, Rosie," said Betsy. "This little mouse isn't going to hurt you."

"Can I have one of those jelly beans?" said Rodney.

"They're not jelly beans," said Betsy. "They're baby mice."

"Baby mice!" the children exclaimed.

"They don't have any eyes," said Rodney.

"They have eyes," said Betsy, "but their eyes aren't open yet. I have a book that says they'll open in ten days."

"They haven't any fur," said Nancy. "Mice have fur."

"They'll get their fur," said Betsy. "Their fur will be just like the mother's."

"Can I have one of those babies?" Rodney asked.

"They belong to my friend Eddie Wilson,"

said Betsy. "Eddie named the mother mouse Bertha."

"I guess I couldn't have a baby mouse," said Rodney, "'cause we have a cat, and I guess cats don't like baby mice. Our cat's going to have babies, too. She's a beautiful cat. She's Angora."

"Let's name the babies," said Nancy.

"Yes, yes!" the children cried.

"But they all look alike," said Betsy. "Tomorrow we won't know one from the other."

The children still insisted on naming the baby mice. "Let's name them after us," said Sammy. "That one next to Bertha's foot is Sammy."

"And the one next to it is Rodney," said Rodney.

"The next one is Nancy," said Nancy.

"And the next one is Jackie," said Jackie.

"Bobo wants one named after him," said Rodney. "So the next one is Bobo."

"Who's Bobo?" Nancy asked.

"Bobo's just make-believe and so is his dog Tinkie," said Fay.

Pointing to the baby mice, Rodney said, "The littlest one is Rosie."

"No, no!" cried Rosie. "I don't want a mouse named after me. I hate mice."

"You have to have one named after you," said Rodney.

"I won't! I won't!" said Rosie, stamping her foot. She went to a chair and sat down.

"OK," said Rodney, "then the little one is Fay."

"Now there are two left," said Betsy.

"Let's name them after the dogs," said Rodney. "Thumpy and Tinkie. Maybe you don't know, but Thumpy is Betsy's dog. Isn't that right, Betsy?"

"That's right," Betsy replied.

"Tinkie isn't a dog," said Sammy. "He's only a make-believe dog."

"He's Bobo's dog," said Rodney.

"Now that you've seen the mice," said Betsy, "go and sit down on your chairs."

The children scrambled for their seats. Nancy was about to sit down on the chair between Rodney and Sammy, but Rodney cried out, "No, No! Bobo's sitting there. Don't sit on Bobo!"

Nancy quickly moved to the seat on the other side of Sammy, and Sammy whispered to her, "Rodney said Tinkie's going to have puppies."

"Oh, maybe we can each have one," said Nancy.

"I don't want a make-believe puppy," said Sammy. "I want a real one."

Just then Betsy called her school to order. "Now, children, I want you to call me Teacher Betsy. Let me hear you say Teacher Betsy."

Five of the children called back, "Teacher Betsy," but Rodney called out, "Go on, you're just Betsy."

Then the others cried, "Yes, yes, you're just Betsy."

Betsy saw that her idea wouldn't work. "All right," she said, "I'm just Betsy."

In the middle of the morning, Betsy went to the refrigerator and brought out six cartons of milk. Then from a box on top of the refrigerator she took out some cookies. She placed a carton in front of each child with two cookies.

Rodney looked at the six cartons of milk. Then he said, "Hey, Betsy, you didn't give Bobo any milk and cookies."

"Oh!" said Betsy. "Does Bobo like milk and cookies?"

" 'Course," Rodney replied.

Betsy placed a carton of milk and two cookies on the table in front of the empty chair between Rodney and Sammy. Then Rodney said, "You didn't put down a cookie for Tinkie."

"Oh!" said Betsy. "Does Tinkie like cookies?"

"Sure," said Rodney.

Betsy placed another cookie on the table.

Soon the children were busy drinking their milk and munching the cookies. Betsy watched Rodney out of the corner of her eye. When he had finished his carton of milk, he picked up the other one that stood on the table between him and Sammy. Rodney began to drink the milk.

"Hey, Rodney," said Sammy, "that's Bobo's milk."

"I know," said Rodney. "Bobo told me to drink it, 'cause he doesn't want it."

At first Sammy looked surprised. Then he picked up Bobo's cookies and popped one after the other into his mouth. This brought a cry from Rodney. "Sammy, you stole Bobo's cookies."

"I did not," Sammy replied. "Bobo gave them to me. He said he didn't like these cookies."

At that moment Nancy reached out and

picked up the cookie that Betsy had put down
for Tinkie. One bite and it was gone.

"Hey," cried Rodney. "You stole Tinkie's
cookie."

"Well, I gave him a puppy biscuit instead,"
said Nancy.

"What do you mean a puppy biscuit," said
Rodney. "I didn't see any puppy biscuit."

"Oh, it was just a make-believe puppy biscuit.
If you can have a make-believe dog, I can have
a make-believe puppy biscuit, can't I?" Nancy
replied.

Later in the morning Nancy called out, "Oh,
Tinkie piddled on the floor!"

Rodney looked at Nancy with his mouth wide
open. Then he said, "He did not! Tinkie did
not piddle on the floor, Nancy. You can't say
what Tinkie does. I say. Nobody says but me.
Bobo is my friend and Tinkie is Bobo's dog,
and I say everything. Nobody says it but me."

Just before twelve o'clock there was a scratching noise on the door. Betsy opened it a crack. She saw her cocker spaniel, Thumpy, so she opened the door. Thumpy came in. "Here's Thumpy," she called to the children. "He's very friendly, so don't be afraid of him."

The children patted Thumpy. "Thumpy's nicer than a make-believe dog," said Nancy.

"You bet," Sammy agreed.

Thumpy poked around the room, exploring the whole place.

Suddenly Rosie cried out, "Oh, Thumpy just did what Tinkie didn't do."

"Oh," cried Betsy, "I forgot to walk Thumpy this morning. I'll get the mop." Betsy opened the door and brought in the mop.

"I'll mop," said Rodney, taking the mop from Betsy.

"Thank you, Rodney," said Betsy. "Perhaps make-believe dogs are better."

"Well, you don't have to mop with Tinkie," said Rodney. "Not ever."

Late in the afternoon Eddie arrived to pick up the mice. He looked at the babies with great interest. He too thought they looked like pink jelly beans.

"The children named them," said Betsy, "but no one can tell which is which. We only know there isn't one named Rosie. Rosie wouldn't have one named after her. She said she hates mice."

" 'Magine that," said Eddie. "I love little field mice. It will be fun to see these little ones grow up."

"Will you bring them back when their eyes are open to show the children?" Betsy asked.

"Oh, sure," Eddie replied. "I'll show them to each of the kids."

"But not to Rosie," said Betsy.

## Chapter 5

# THE FOURTH OF JULY
# PICNIC

BETSY and the children had been invited to
a Fourth of July picnic lunch by the neighbors, Mr. and Mrs. Jackson, who lived next
door. The Jacksons had a big swimming pool,
and they told Betsy that she and the children
could all have a swim after lunch.

When the time came to go to the Jacksons',

the children changed into their swimming suits. Each one had a towel over his arm.

Betsy said, "Now we'll have a little Fourth of July parade and march over to Mr. and Mrs. Jackson's."

"We need a band to play music for a parade," said Fay.

"There's a toy drum here someone can use," said Betsy.

"I can beat the drum," said Sammy, who was holding his chicken. "Here, Betsy," he said, "you carry my chicken, and I'll beat the drum."

"This chicken is a nuisance," said Betsy. "How can I hand out American flags if I have to hold a chicken?"

"Well, I'll put Mona down," said Sammy. "She'll follow me." Sammy put down the chicken and picked up the drum.

"I can play a comb with a piece of tissue paper over it," said Rosie. Betsy took a comb out of the closet and brought it to Rosie. In a moment, she began to make some sounds with it.

Betsy began to hand out little American flags. She gave a flag to each child, and then Rodney said, "You didn't give Bobo a flag."

"Oh," said Betsy, "where is Bobo?"

"He's right in front of me," said Rodney. "Give the flag to me, and I'll give it to him."

Betsy handed another flag to Rodney, and Rodney said, "Bobo says I can carry it for him." Rodney held the two flags in his left hand.

"Now follow me," said Betsy to the children.

"Can I be first?" Rodney asked.

"With two flags, you can be first behind me," Betsy replied.

"The band should go first," said Sammy.

"Very well," said Betsy. "You and Rosie can walk in front of me."

Sammy and Rosie stepped in front of Betsy, and so did the chicken.

The children walked out the door and started off for the Jacksons'. As Rodney passed the sandbox, he picked up a bucket. It was painted red, white, and blue. "This is going to be my soldier hat," he said, and he put the bucket on his head with the handle under his chin.

*Bang! Bang! Bang!* went the drum.

As the parade marched across the garden and climbed over the wall that separated the two houses, the children could see Mr. and Mrs. Jackson on their terrace. Star and Lillybell and Billy Porter were there too. Mr. Jackson was standing beside a grill.

"I know what!" Sammy cried out. "We're going to have hamburgers!"

Sammy's words quickly spread to the other children, and they all cried out, "Hamburgers! Hamburgers! Hamburgers!"

When they reached Mr. Jackson and could

see the red coals, Mr. Jackson said, "Sorry, kids! No hamburgers. It's hot dogs."

"Hot dogs!" Sammy cried out. "They're OK."

All the children agreed that hot dogs were OK.

Suddenly Rodney cried out, "I can't see!"

"Well, take that bucket off your head," said Betsy.

Rodney took hold of the bucket. Then he shouted, "I can't get it off!"

Betsy tried to get it off, but it seemed to be stuck fast.

"Oh, I can't see! I can't see!" Rodney cried. "The bucket is over my eyes."

In a moment everyone knew that Rodney couldn't see, for he bumped into the table on which Mrs. Jackson had placed a large box full of hot dogs and a great big blueberry pie. Just as everyone cried out, "Look out!" the table went over and everything fell to the ground.

Thumpy, who had joined the party, lost no time reaching the hot dogs, which were scattered among the pieces of pie on the grass. He gobbled up three of them and ran off with two in his mouth.

Star ran after Thumpy. "Thumpy, drop them! Drop them, Thumpy!"

Betsy ran after Star. "Star," she cried, "let him have them. We don't want hot dogs that have been in Thumpy's mouth. I just hope he chokes."

"He will," Billy called out. "Then he'll throw up. I know cocker spaniels. They're the greatest for throwing up."

Nancy called out, "Some of these hot dogs have blueberry pie all over them, and some have dirt and grass stuck on them."

When Betsy saw what had happened to the

hot dogs and the pie, she left Rodney jumping up and down with his bucket on his head and ran to her mother. She told her about the catastrophe that had happened to their lunch.

"I think I can help," said her mother. "I have a big package of hamburger, which I bought at the market yesterday. Take it over to Mr. Jackson, and you can all have hamburgers."

"Oh, Mother, thank you!" cried Betsy.

Betsy climbed over the wall again and ran toward Mr. Jackson. As she ran she called out, "Here's hamburger! Hamburger! Hamburger!"

"Hurrah!" cried some of the children. "Hamburger!"

"Didn't I say we were going to have hamburgers?" said Sammy.

Rodney was still screaming and tugging at the bucket. "I can't get it off! I can't get it off!" he cried.

Betsy took hold of the bucket and tried to get it off. It seemed to be stuck fast. Then Mr. Jackson came and tried to take it off, but without success.

"What'll I do! What'll I do!" Rodney cried.

"I'll call the police," said Mr. Jackson. "Maybe they can help us." Mr. Jackson went into the house to make the telephone call.

In about five minutes a red police car drove into the Jacksons' driveway, and to Betsy's delight Mr. Kilpatrick stepped out. When he saw the situation, he said, "I think I can take care of that. I have a pair of shears here in the car that will cut metal. Just a minute, young fellow," he added. "I'll have you out of that in a jiffy. Just stand still. I don't want to cut off your ear."

"Oh, oh!" Rodney cried out, as Mr. Kilpatrick set to work. "I can feel you cutting off my ear."

"I'm nowhere near your ear," said Mr. Kilpatrick. "It's nothing but your imagination. Hold still, or I'll cut your whole head off."

Rodney held still while Mr. Kilpatrick worked on the bucket. "It's this deep ridge about two inches below the edge of the bucket that is the problem," said Mr. Kilpatrick. "After I cut up through the bucket, I can separate the parts and you'll be free."

Rodney stood still, and only once did he say, "Hurry up, Mr. Kilpatrick!" All the children and Betsy stood by, watching. When Mr. Kilpatrick finally lifted the bucket off Rodney's head, Rodney gave a sigh of relief and rubbed his forehead. "It hurts," he said.

Mrs. Jackson looked at Rodney's head. Then she went into the house and came back with a jar of vaseline. "This will be good for it," she said, smoothing the salve on the red bruise. "The skin isn't broken," she added. "It will be better soon."

The children all seemed relieved that Rodney was free from the bucket.

"Thank you, Mrs. Jackson," said Rodney.

At last Mr. Jackson called out, "The hamburgers are ready, so all of you come and sit down on the grass. The picnic is about to begin, and I hope Mr. Kilpatrick will join us."

"That I will," said Mr. Kilpatrick.

Everyone sat down on the grass, and soon Mr. Kilpatrick, with the children gathered around him, was enjoying the Fourth of July picnic with hamburgers on buns. For dessert they had ice cream, which Mrs. Jackson had in her freezer.

When Mr. Kilpatrick got up to leave, he said, "Thanks for the picnic. Now Rodney, you be careful what you stick your head into. All the men in the police force are not as careful with cutters as I am, and you may get your head cut off. You'd look mighty funny carrying your head around under your arm."

Everyone laughed and waved to Mr. Kilpatrick as he got back into his car. Then the children jumped into the pool with Mr. and Mrs. Jackson and had a wonderful swim.

# Chapter 6

# POOR MONA

I T WAS a morning shortly after the Fourth of
July. Betsy had just given Rodney the rub-
ber blocks so that he could build a castle, the
crayons to Rosie, who wanted to color pictures
in a book, jars of paint to Jackie and Fay so that
they could do some finger painting.

Betsy looked around at the children, and then

96

she said, "I wonder where Sammy is this morning?"

As soon as the words were out of her mouth, they could hear a child crying. The crying came from some way up the street, and it grew louder and louder.

"Betsy, somebody's crying," said Fay. "Do you hear somebody crying?"

"Indeed, I do," Betsy replied.

Soon the door opened, and Lillybell led Sammy into the room. Now everyone knew who was crying. It was Sammy. In his arms he carried his pet chicken, Mona. There were tears running down Sammy's cheeks, and there was blood on his shirt. His shoulders shook with sobbing.

"Oh!" cried Betsy. "What happened?"

Sammy went right on crying, but Lillybell spoke up. "Sammy's chicken was following us, and when she got into the center of the street, a car came very fast and hit her. I guess she's dead." Lillybell started to cry too.

"Oh!" cried all of the children.

"That's terrible," said Rodney. "The poor chicken."

Betsy put her arm around Sammy and said, "I'm so sorry, Sammy. I know how much you loved that chicken." Betsy reached out and said, "Shall I take her, Sammy?"

"No," Sammy replied, "I want to hold her."

"Very well," said Betsy, wiping the tears from Sammy's face with her handkerchief. "Don't cry anymore, Sammy. Your daddy will give you another chicken for a pet."

"But I love Mona. I don't want another chicken." Sammy cried louder than ever.

All of the children gathered around Sammy. "The poor chicken! Poor Mona!" they murmured.

Nancy put out her hands and smoothed

Mona's feathers. There were tears in Nancy's eyes. "Such a pretty chicken," she said.

Fay wanted to comfort Sammy. "I had a rabbit once," she said. "I got it for Easter, and one day a dog killed it. I loved my rabbit, and I cried awful hard. But do you know what? One day I looked out the window, and there sitting in our yard was a beautiful black-and-white rabbit. My daddy put her in the rabbit hutch, and now I just love that rabbit. I named her Happy, because I was so happy when I saw her."

Sammy had stopped crying and was looking at Fay with his big brown eyes still swimming in tears. "Where did she come from?" he asked Fay.

"I don't know," Fay replied. "She was just there. Daddy took her picture and put it in the paper to see if anybody had lost a black-and-white rabbit. But nobody called us, so we still have Happy. Don't cry, Sammy. You'll get another pet. Just keep looking out the window."

Sammy held the chicken up to Betsy. "What shall we do with her?" he asked.

Rodney ran forward. "Why can't your mother cook her?" he said.

Sammy went off into another crying spell.

"Oh, Rodney, Sammy couldn't eat his pet!" said Betsy.

Then Rosie spoke up. "My granddaddy has a big bird. It's beautiful. It was alive once, but now it's stuffed. It looks just like real. Maybe you could get Mona stuffed."

"I don't want a stuffed chicken," said Sammy. "I want a real live chicken."

Betsy wiped Sammy's eyes again with her handkerchief. "Would you like to have me bury Mona in the yard?" she asked. Sammy nodded his head.

Betsy found a cardboard box into which she placed Mona. Then she went out into the yard and, taking a spade from among her father's garden tools, dug a hole near the rosebed. Finally she called out to Sammy, "Bring the box." Sammy brought the box, and Betsy told him to place it in the hole. The rest of the children gathered around and watched. Betsy shoveled dirt back over the box and tamped it down.

"Mona must have flowers, Sammy," said Nancy. "We must get some flowers."

"Yes, flowers," said Jackie.

The children went to a nearby flower bed and began to pick petunias, which they placed around the edge of the grave. Sammy walked to a rosebush and picked a red rose. He stuck it upright in the earth right on top of Mona's grave.

"Come now," Betsy said to the children, "get back inside and go on with all those lovely things you were doing." The children ran inside. Fay made room for Sammy at the table and helped him with his finger painting.

Late in the morning, not long before the time came for the children to go home, Betsy said, "Now I'm going to tell you a story."

"What's it about?" Rodney asked.

"It's the story of the Little Red Hen," said Betsy.

Sammy again burst into tears. "I don't want to hear about a little red hen. I want to hear about a little white chicken."

"I want to hear the story of Chicken Little," Rosie cried out.

"I don't want to hear 'Chicken Little,'" said Rodney. "I want to hear about a horse, and Bobo wants to hear about a horse. Bobo and I like horses."

Betsy, changing the subject, said, "I'll tell you the story called 'Jack and the Beanstalk.'"

"Did he have a white chicken?" Sammy asked.

"Now let me think," said Betsy, putting her

hand to her head. In a moment, she said, "I think he did have a white chicken. Yes, it was a white chicken that found a big bean in Mr. McGregor's garden."

Rosie called out, "I remember Mr. McGregor. He owned the garden where Peter Rabbit used to go."

"Well," said Betsy, "this white chicken didn't eat the big bean, but brought it to Jack and Jack planted it. Soon it began to grow, and it grew and grew until it was so big Jack could climb up the beanstalk to the very top. On his way he picked great big, fat beans, which he put in his pocket. When Jack got to the top of the beanstalk, he could look over the garden wall and he could see the whole world."

"What happened to the white chicken?" Sammy asked.

Betsy continued. "When Jack climbed down the beanstalk, he gave his chicken all of the big beans he had in his pocket, and yum, yum, did she like those beans. Afterward she laid golden eggs for Jack."

Rodney spoke up. "I go to story hour at the library," he said, "and the librarian told us the story of Jack and the Beanstalk, but it wasn't like your story. There was a giant, she told us, and the chicken that laid the golden eggs belonged to the giant."

"That's right," said Fay. "I go to story hour, too. You didn't say, 'Fee, fi, fo, fum.'"

"That's right," said Rodney. "The giant said, 'Fee, fi, fo, fum, I smell the blood of an Englishman.' That was when Jack was in the oven. Your Jack didn't go into the oven, Betsy."

"Well, that was a different Jack," said Betsy.

Rodney whispered to Fay, "I don't think Betsy knows the story of Jack and the Beanstalk. She's mixed up."

"I like 'Fee, fi, fo, fum,'" said Sammy.

Then all the children called out, "Fee, fi, fo, fum."

"I'd like to have a chicken that laid golden eggs," said Sammy. "My father's chickens just lay chicken's eggs, but maybe someday he'll get one that lays golden eggs."

# Chapter 7

# WHAT SAMMY SAW
# OUT THE WINDOW

ONE MORNING Rodney was late. The children kept saying to Betsy, "Rodney's late!"

"I know," Betsy replied each time.

Again and again the children ran to the door, looking for Rodney.

Finally Sammy climbed up on a bench to look

out the window. He kept saying, "He hasn't come yet." Suddenly Sammy cried out, "Oh, a white kitten just ran into the yard. It's sitting in the grass. It looks like a snowball." Sammy got down from the bench and ran to the door.

All of the children wanted to see the white kitten. Some went to the door. Others climbed up on the bench to look out the window.

Sammy ran out into the yard, calling back, "I'm going to get that kitten!"

At that very moment Betsy, who had joined the children at the window, saw Rodney come into the yard. Sammy and Rodney met beside the kitten. Rodney picked up the kitten. Sammy's face fell. Betsy heard him say, "I saw it first."

"I saw it first," said Rodney. "It's my cat's kitten."

"Oh," said Sammy. "It's a pretty kitten."

"Yes," said Rodney. Then he handed the kitten to Sammy and said, "I was bringing it to you when it jumped out of my arms and ran away."

"Honest?" said Sammy. "You mean it's for me, really?"

"That's right," said Rodney. " 'Course it isn't a white chicken, but it's a white kitten."

Sammy held the kitten in his arms. He snuggled it up to his cheek and said, "It's the prettiest kitten I ever saw. Thank you. I'll call it Snowball, because that's what it looks like."

All of the children gathered around Sammy, wanting to pat Snowball. They were full of questions. "How many kittens did your cat have?" "Are all of the kittens white?" "Can I have a kitten?"

Rodney replied, "Our cat had three kittens. There were two white ones and a black-and-white one."

"Oh, can I have the other white one?" Rosie asked.

"No," Rodney replied, "because we gave it to

the man who lives next door to us. He wanted to give it to his granddaughter. He said she was crazy to have a white kitten."

"What are you going to do with the black-and-white one?" Jackie asked.

"We're keeping it," said Rodney. "It's real cute."

Sammy was overjoyed with his kitten. "You see," said Fay, "didn't I tell you to look out the window? I told you, remember? I looked out the window and saw my rabbit."

Sammy laughed. "Yes," he said, "and I looked out the window and saw my kitten."

Sammy carried Snowball into the schoolroom, and the rest of the children followed. He sat on the floor with the kitten in his arms, but the kitten soon jumped away from him. He began to rush around the room, up on the table, onto the chairs, up on the windowsill, and finally on the top of the refrigerator. Betsy said, "I think you should have named this kitten Frisky. I never knew such a lively kitten."

Betsy had gone to the store early that morning to get the children's milk, which she brought home in a large paper bag. She had put the milk in the refrigerator and the paper bag on the floor behind the refrigerator.

When the time came for the children's milk, Sammy said, "Can Snowball have some milk?"

"Of course," said Betsy. Betsy opened the refrigerator door and took out the small cartons of milk for the children. Then she poured some milk from a larger container into a saucer and set it down for Snowball.

The kitten licked it up while Betsy put a milk carton in front of each child on the big table. As she was opening the cartons the kitten leaped onto the table and, before anyone could stop him, knocked over all the milk. Then Snowball began to lick up the milk while Betsy ran to get some paper towels. Snowball, not satisfied with licking up the milk, also rolled in it. Soon his white fur was wet with milk. When Betsy finished wiping up the table, she wiped up Snowball and put him on the floor.

The children were still waiting for their milk. "I only have a little bit now," Betsy said, "but I'll divide it up among you." She brought each child a paper cup with a little milk.

After a while Sammy looked around for Snowball. The kitten was nowhere in sight. "Where's Snowball?" Sammy cried out. "Where's Snowball?"

Everyone began to look for the kitten. They looked under the table, under the chairs, and under the bench by the window.

Sammy began to cry. "I want Snowball," he said, sobbing. "I lost Mona, and now I lost Snowball."

"Don't cry," said Betsy. "He can't be very far away."

Then the children heard the rattling of paper. Betsy ran and pulled the paper bag out from behind the refrigerator. "Why, here's Snowball!" she said. "He was inside the paper bag."

The children laughed, and Sammy dried his tears. He hugged his kitten, but finally he put Snowball down on the floor. Snowball spent a long time licking himself all over.

This morning the children were going to paint, so Betsy brought the paint jars out on the table. There were jars of red, blue, green, and yellow paint. Before long the kitten was on the table again.

"See how careful Snowball is?" said Sammy. "See how he walks around the paint jars?"

Snowball didn't walk carefully very long. Soon he began to frisk around and knock the jars of paint over. Where the milk had been, now

there were puddles of paint. Snowball didn't try
to eat the paint; he just walked in it. Soon his
paws were covered with paint. At last he sat
down and began to rub his ears with his paws.
Red, blue, green, and yellow paint was smeared
on his ears and on the top of his head. The children cried out, "Look at Snowball!"

Betsy picked up the kitten and with a paper
towel wiped his fur. Now all of the colors were
smeared together. "He looks like a finger painting!" said Rosie.

"Can you wash him, Betsy?" Sammy asked.

"Well, cats don't like to have baths," said
Betsy, "but he can't stay like this forever."

Betsy took Snowball into the little washroom.
She ran water into the washbasin and carefully
bathed the kitten. Snowball kept meowing all
through the bath. When Betsy finished, she held
him up and said, "You just be glad I'm not going

to hang you on the line by your ears with clothes-
pins!"

At last Betsy handed Snowball to Sammy and
said, "Sammy, I think you had better take Snowball out in the yard. I don't have any litter pan
for him."

"You mean you think Snowball has to go to
the bathroom?" Sammy asked.

"Maybe," said Betsy, "after all he did drink a
lot of milk." She opened the screen door, and
Sammy took Snowball outside.

They hadn't been out very long, when Sammy
called out, "Betsy, Snowball went to the bathroom, but now he's hiding. I can't find him."

"I think Tinkie chased him," said Rodney.
"Tinkie always chases cats."

Sammy kept crying out, "I can't find him! I
can't find him!"

"Come, children," said Betsy, "we'll have to
find Snowball. What a nuisance this kitten is!"

The children followed Betsy into the yard. They looked around the garage and under all the bushes, but Snowball was not there. Betsy and the children ran down the driveway. They looked all around the neighbors' houses. Betsy even looked up into the trees. "It would be just like that kitten to run up a tree," she said to herself, but she didn't see any white kitten in a tree.

Sammy ran all the way to the corner. There, coming up the sidewalk, he saw a girl, about Betsy's age, carrying a white kitten. "That's my kitten," said Sammy.

"It certainly is not your kitten," said the girl. "It's my kitten. She's been lost for two days, and I just found her."

"That's my kitten," said Sammy, "that's Snowball."

"It's not," said the girl. "This kitten is named Lollipop."

Then Betsy arrived. "Betsy," said Sammy,

"this girl says that's her kitten. It isn't, is it? It's Snowball."

Betsy knew the girl, and she said, "Hello, Sandra. I'm afraid this kitten is Sammy's. It just ran away, and we've been looking for it."

"I'm sorry, Betsy," said Sandra, "but this is my kitten, Lollipop. I just found her. She's been lost for two days."

"Well," said Betsy, "I think we can find out whether it's Snowball or Lollipop. I had to bathe Snowball a little while ago, because he got paint on himself. Let's see if there is any sign of paint still on his fur."

"Well, I know this is Lollipop," said Sandra, but she handed the kitten to Betsy.

Betsy looked at the kitten's paws, but there was no sign of paint. Then she looked over the rest of him carefully. All the while she was saying to herself, "Oh, Snowball, please show some paint, a little blue or a speck of yellow." But

Snowball appeared to be clean. There was nothing to see but pure white fur and a pink nose. Then she looked into his ears, and there she spotted a tiny smudge of blue paint. "Oh, Snowball," she said, "now I know who you are." Then she said to Sandra, "See, there is some blue paint in his ear. This is surely Snowball."

"Oh, dear!" said Sandra. "Where is Lollipop? I just got her last week. My granddad gave her to me for my birthday, but she's been lost for two days." Tears began to flow from Sandra's eyes.

"Oh, dear," she cried. "She's the dearest kitten. She's the sweetest kitten. Now maybe I'll never find her again. Oh where, oh where is she?"

Rodney, who had just joined Betsy and Sandra, heard what Sandra had said to Betsy. "Where does your granddad live, Sandra?" he asked. When Sandra told him, Rodney clapped his hands together. "Your granddad lives next door to us, and we gave the other white kitten to him." Rodney laughed. "Your Lollipop is one of our cat's kittens. She's Snowball's sister."

"Oh, I wish I could find her," said Sandra.

"We'll help you find Lollipop," said Betsy, "but first of all Sammy must put Snowball back into the schoolroom, so we don't lose him again." Sammy ran back to Betsy's with Snowball.

Betsy asked, "Have you looked up into the trees, Sandra? Kittens are always climbing trees, and they can never get down."

Sandra started looking up into the trees, but she didn't see any kitten. Betsy and the children looked under the bushes for Lollipop. Finally Betsy came upon a place in the lawn where there was an open drainpipe. She stooped down and looked into it, and she heard a very faint meow. "Oh, Sandra," she called out. "I think your kitten is in this pipe."

Sandra stooped down and called, "Here, kitty, kitty, kitty!" No kitty appeared. The faint cry continued. "Oh, why doesn't she come out?" said Sandra, almost in tears.

"I guess she doesn't know how," said Betsy.

Rodney stooped down and looked into the pipe. "I bet she'd come out if you had some fish," he said.

"I bet she would," Betsy agreed.

"Well, I'll get some," said Sandra, rushing back to her house.

Before long she was back with some tuna fish. She put it at the opening of the pipe and called, "Here, kitty, kitty. Here's fish, kitty." Lollipop popped out and ate the fish. Then Sandra picked her up and said, "You're a naughty kitten to run away and hide!"

Sammy came to Betsy and said, "Don't you like Snowball, Betsy?"

"I like kittens," said Betsy, "but today there've been too many kittens."

"I looked out the window the way Fay said,

and I saw my beautiful white kitten," said
Sammy.

"Don't look again," said Betsy. "I wouldn't
want you to see a white elephant!"

# Chapter 8

## EDDIE'S MICE

Betsy had promised to take the children to
the zoo, and her mother had agreed to
drive them there. The day had been selected, and
the children were looking forward to seeing the
animals. Then, the week before, the newspaper
announced that the zoo would be closed for the
month of August in order to make some repairs.

Betsy, as well as the children, was disappointed. The morning before they had expected to go to the zoo, however, the telephone rang at Betsy's house. Betsy could hear it ringing up in the hall. She heard her mother's footsteps as she went to answer it.

In a few moments Betsy's mother called down the basement stairs. "Betsy, Eddie Wilson wants to speak to you. He says it's important."

Betsy ran up the stairs. She picked up the telephone. "Hi, Eddie!"

"Hi, Betsy!" Eddie replied. "You know those baby mice?"

"Sure," said Betsy.

"Well, they're all grown up now, and my mother says I have to get rid of them. She says she can't stand having all these mice around here. She says I should drown them, but I can't drown those little things, 'specially since your kids named them after themselves. 'Course, they all look alike, so I can't tell Nancy from Sammy, but anyway I can't drown them."

"Well, what are you going to do with them?" Betsy asked.

"I'm coming to that," Eddie replied. "That's why I'm calling you."

"Well, get on with it, Eddie," said Betsy. "I've left the children alone."

"It's like this," said Eddie. "I can't put these mice out in my mother's garden."

"'Course not," said Betsy.

"So," said Eddie, "I'm going to take them out to the country and let them go free in some open field. After all, they *are* field mice."

"What about Bertha, the mother?" Betsy asked.

Eddie groaned. "Oh, I guess she has to go too," he said. "I can't bear it. She's such a nice pet. She knows her name and comes when I call her."

"Well, it's too bad," said Betsy, "but where do I come into this?"

"I thought you and the kids might like to go along. My mother said she'll take us in our station wagon," said Eddie.

"Oh, that's great, Eddie," Betsy said. "We were going to the zoo, but it's closed. I'm sure the children would be delighted to go. I'll bring sandwiches."

"OK," said Eddie. "We'll pick you up tomorrow morning about eleven o'clock."

"We'll be ready," said Betsy, as she hung up the telephone.

When she rejoined the children, she told them of Eddie's offer. The children were very pleased.

The following morning, when the children arrived, Betsy had a large loaf of bread and a jar of peanut butter on the table. "I'm going to make sandwiches to take with us," she said.

"Oh, goody!" said Fay.

"Are they going to be peanut butter and jelly?" Jackie asked.

"I'll get some jelly," said Betsy, and she ran upstairs to the kitchen.

When she came back, Nancy said, "Is it grape jelly?"

Betsy looked at the label on the jar. "No," she said, "it's currant jelly."

"I only like grape jelly," said Nancy.

Then Rodney spoke up. "Is that chunky peanut butter?" he asked.

"No, it isn't chunky peanut butter," Betsy replied.

"I only like chunky peanut butter," said Rodney.

"I don't want any peanut butter," said Rosie. "I just like crab-apple jelly on my bread."

"There isn't any crab-apple jelly," said Betsy.

"Well, we have crab-apple jelly at our house," said Rosie.

"Then you'll have to eat your bread and jelly at your house," said Betsy, "and you'll miss going with us and the mice."

"I'll go home and get a jar of crab-apple jelly," said Rosie.

"Oh, no," said Betsy. "There is plenty of jelly here."

"But it isn't crab-apple jelly," said Rosie. "I can get it from Maggie." Rosie ran out the door.

"Now, Rodney," said Betsy, "I hope you're not going home to get chunky peanut butter."

"Oh, I'll eat that old stuff you have there," said Rodney. "Just put it on thick."

"Very well," said Betsy. "I'll have to put everyone's name on these sandwiches. You're all so fussy."

Before long Rosie was back. She came running into the yard with the jar of jelly in her hands. "Here's the crab-apple jelly," she cried out at the top of her voice.

Just as she reached the door she dropped the jar. It crashed to the cement walk and broke. The jelly splashed out and lay with the pieces of broken jar on the sidewalk. Thumpy ran to the jelly, but Betsy called out, "No, Thumpy! You might cut your tongue on the broken glass." She grabbed hold of Thumpy's collar and pulled him away from the jelly. Then she picked up the pieces of glass. "Now," she said to Thumpy, releasing him, "go ahead and enjoy yourself." Thumpy did. He cleared up all the jelly and licked his chops.

Then Rosie cried out, "Oh, there's jelly on my new white shoes. I'll have to run home to Maggie and get her to clean my shoes."

"I'll clean your shoes," said Betsy.

"Oh, that's nice," said Rosie, taking her shoes off.

Betsy set to work cleaning Rosie's shoes with

white shoe cleaner while the children played in the yard.

In a few minutes Fay came in to Betsy with a long string of blue yarn in her hand.

"Now what is it?" Betsy asked.

"I caught my sleeve on a hook in the wall," Fay replied, "and I pulled the string. I guess I shouldn't have pulled it, 'cause I unknitted it, didn't I?"

"That's too bad, Fay," said Betsy, "but your mother will fix it." Then Betsy said to herself, "I've made sandwiches, I've cleaned shoes, but I'm not going to knit a sweater."

Just then Eddie arrived. "Hi, Betsy!" he said. "How are you doing?"

"Just fine," Betsy replied. "I hope you're not fussy about peanut-butter sandwiches."

"Oh, no," Eddie replied. "Just as long as they're made with raisin bread. A little bacon is nice too."

"You can go drown in a lake," said Betsy. "I haven't any raisin bread, and I'm not going to fry bacon."

Eddie laughed. "I was just kidding," he said.

The children all gathered around the table. "Where are the mice? Where are the mice?" they called out.

"They're in the car," Eddie replied.

The children rushed to the car followed by Eddie and Betsy. Mrs. Wilson was at the driver's wheel. The children scrambled in, calling out, "We want to see the mice! Where are the mice?"

"They're in the cage on the floor of the car," she replied.

The children knelt down to look in the cage. "Oh, aren't they cute!" they said.

"Which one is named after me?" Jackie asked Eddie.

"I don't know," said Eddie. "They all look alike."

"I think it's this one," said Jackie, pointing to the one with the biggest ears.

"Oh, that's Big Ears," said Eddie.

"Where's the mother mouse, Bertha?" Nancy asked.

Eddie pointed to Bertha. "I can't bear to let Bertha go," he said with a sigh.

Then Mrs. Wilson called and said, "Betsy, you and Eddie come in the front with me."

Betsy and Eddie got into the front seat with Mrs. Wilson. Betsy held the bag with the sandwiches on her lap.

Mrs. Wilson headed the car away from the town and out into the country. "Now, children," said Betsy, "keep your eyes open. We have to find a good spot to let those mice out." All the children started looking, and every once in a while one of them would call out, "There's a nice place."

But Eddie would say, "No, that's not a nice field. We have to find a better place."

Sometimes Betsy would cry out, "There's a good spot!"

But each time Eddie would say, "No, not there!"

Finally Betsy said, "Eddie, you're as fussy about this field as the children were about their peanut-butter sandwiches."

"Well, I want these little mice to be happy when I let them out," said Eddie.

Betsy laughed. "Maybe you better show them the place and talk it over with them."

"You're just being fresh," said Eddie.

Suddenly Mrs. Wilson turned to Betsy and said, "Betsy, I can smell those cheese sandwiches right through the paper bag."

"They're not cheese sandwiches," Betsy replied. "They're peanut butter and jelly."

"Well, I seem to be smelling cheese," said Mrs. Wilson.

Eddie coughed, but he said nothing.

Finally, when they were far out into the country surrounded by open fields, Mrs. Wilson said, "This is it! I'm not going any farther."

"Well, let's eat," said Eddie.

His mother said, "Eddie, you don't want to get rid of these mice. That's what's the matter."

"Well, can't we eat first?" said Eddie. "I'm hungry."

"Very well," said Mrs. Wilson, "let's eat. But this is where we get rid of those mice."

"Are we having a picnic?" Fay asked.

"Of course," Betsy replied. "Haven't we brought sandwiches? Sandwiches are always a picnic."

Mrs. Wilson and the children got out of the car, and they soon found a lovely spot under some trees. They all sat down, and Betsy opened

the paper bag and handed out the sandwiches. "I hope you each get the one you ordered," she said, "and I hope Mrs. Wilson will like hers."

Mrs. Wilson laughed. "Thank you, Betsy," she said. "What a lot you've done for these children."

"Oh, it's fun," said Betsy.

After they ate the sandwiches, Mrs. Wilson said, "Now, Eddie, the mice! Get rid of them!"

"Oh, Mom, do I have to get rid of them?" Eddie moaned.

"Have to?" said Mrs. Wilson. "That's why I've driven you all these miles. Now get on with it. Those mice will be a lot happier in the field than they are in that cage."

But the mice didn't seem to want to go. Instead, they crawled over Eddie, sniffing at his pockets. Mrs. Wilson watched them. Then she said, "Eddie, do you have anything in your pockets that would attract these mice?"

"Just a little bit of cheese," he said.

"So that's what I've been smelling," said his mother.

"It's just a little last goody for them," said Eddie.

"Well, give it to them, or they'll never leave," said Mrs. Wilson.

Eddie took the cheese out of his pockets and broke it up, giving each mouse a bit. Then he pushed them off into the grass, but the mice didn't want to go. They kept poking at his pockets. Finally each child, except Rosie, shoved a mouse and started it off into the grass.

When all of the mice had disappeared, everyone got back into the car and Mrs. Wilson started for home. They hadn't gone far, however, when she looked down at Eddie and saw the head of a little mouse sticking out of his pocket.

She stopped the car. "Eddie Wilson!" she cried. "You have a mouse in your pocket!"

Eddie felt in his pocket and pulled out Bertha. "Honest, Mom, I didn't know she was there. Honest, I didn't. She must have crawled in. I guess she thought I had more cheese."

"I'm not going back," said his mother. "You'll have to let her go right here."

"Oh, Mom, I can't let her go here, all by herself. She'll be so lonesome. Please, can't I take her back home with us? She's so little and cute. Think how she'll miss me and her children if she's here all by herself."

Mrs. Wilson started the car. "All right," she said, "but if she has any more babies, out she goes."

"She won't have any more babies," said Eddie. "I promise you, no more babies."

# *Chapter 9*

# TOBY'S GRADUATION DAY

LITTLE JACKIE talked a great deal about her dog Toby, who was going to Obedience School. "My Toby is a good dog," she would say. "My Toby is obedient." But more than anything Jackie liked to say, "My Toby is going to graduate." Jackie liked the word *graduate*.

One day Betsy's mother asked her to do an

errand for her. As the store was near Jackie's house, Betsy walked home with Jackie after school. When they reached Jackie's house, Betsy went up on the porch and rang the bell.

Once again terrible barking began, and in a moment Toby was jumping at the door, seeming as if he might break it down. When Jackie's mother came to the door, Betsy could hear her saying, "Down, Toby, down! Be quiet, Toby!" Toby went right on barking and scratching on the door. Several minutes passed before Mrs. Oakie could open the door. When she did she said, "Oh, that dog!"

"I thought he was going to Obedience School," said Betsy. "Jackie's always saying how good he is and that he's going to graduate. Jackie just loves the word *graduate*."

"Well, I don't know," said Mrs. Oakie. "Maybe he's good in school, but I don't see any improvement here at home."

"Oh, Toby's a good dog," said Jackie. "When is he going to graduate, Mommy?"

"Two weeks from next Saturday is the day," her mother answered, "and I hope by then he will have made friends with the great Dane that Toby doesn't seem to like."

"I hope the great Dane likes Toby," said Betsy.

"From what I've seen, I'm not too sure," said Mrs. Oakie.

Betsy laughed. "Oh, dear!" she said.

"Why don't you come to graduation, Betsy?" Mrs. Oakie said. "It costs fifty cents, because the school is raising money for the S.P.C.A."

"What's the S.P.C.A., Mommy?" Jackie asked.

"The Society for the Prevention of Cruelty to Animals," her mother replied.

"I'd like to go," said Betsy.

"They're going to have a door prize," said Mrs. Oakie. "It's a little puppy. A poodle."

Jackie's next question was, "What's a door prize?"

Her mother explained, "When you go in, you get half a ticket at the door with a number on it. Then before you go home, all the other halves of the tickets with the same numbers are put into a big jar or basket. Somebody pulls out one ticket and reads out the number. The person with the number called wins the prize."

"Oh, Mommy," Jackie cried, "do you think that I might win the poodle?"

"If you do, we'll give it away!" her mother replied. "One dog is enough around here."

As Betsy walked home from the store she kept thinking of the poodle. She knew someone who needed the poodle very badly. It was Rodney.

Rodney needed a real live Tinkie! Betsy decided to take Rodney and the rest of the children with her to the graduation. Maybe Rodney would win the poodle. At least there was a chance.

When Betsy reached home, she telephoned all the children's mothers and told them of her plan. All the mothers said their children could go.

The following day, when the children came to school, Rodney and Rosie talked excitedly at the same time, telling Betsy all about the graduation day, as though Betsy didn't know anything about it. "My mommy says maybe I'll come home with the poodle," said Rodney. "Then I'll have a poodle just like Tinkie."

"Don't count on it, Rodney," said Betsy.

Betsy began to worry. Suppose one of the other children won the puppy instead of Rodney? That would be a problem. Well, she would just hope that didn't happen. She did so want Rodney to get that poodle.

The children could hardly wait for the day to come. Every day at least one would say to Betsy, "Is it tomorrow we go to see the dogs?"

And Betsy would say, "No, not tomorrow." But finally the day came when she could answer, "Yes, tomorrow we go to see the dogs."

Jackie piped up, "That's the day Toby is going to graduate."

At two o'clock on Saturday afternoon, Betsy and all the children but Jackie gathered together. Jackie was going with her mother and Toby on a leash. It wasn't far to the Obedience School, so Betsy and the children walked. On the way many people with their own dogs on leashes passed the children.

Rodney admired a great Dane and said to Betsy, "I like that big dog, but I like poodles better."

Betsy looked at the great Dane and thought to herself, I guess that's the dog Toby doesn't like.

When Betsy and the children reached the door of the building, there were a great many dogs on leashes, and there was a great deal of barking. Slowly a line of people passed through the door in spite of the yapping dogs. At last Betsy handed the money for the admission to the man in attendance. He gave her some tickets and said, "Hold on to these for the door prize." The man pointed to a box on the floor. "Take a look at the prize here in this box."

Betsy and the children looked into the box. There was a dear little poodle puppy—as black as coal. "Oh!" Rodney cried out. "That's just the kind of a poodle I want. He's exactly like Tinkie. Can I take him home with me?"

"He isn't yours, Rodney," said Betsy, "but here's your ticket. If the number on it is drawn,

you will win the puppy. Somebody will win it."

"If you get it, Betsy, will you give it to me?" Rodney asked.

"I promise you I will," said Betsy. "I have Thumpy at home, and Mother says I can't have another dog."

Betsy gave each of the children a ticket and told them not to lose them. "You have to show it in order to claim the puppy."

"I won't lose it!" came as a chorus from the children. They were all holding their tickets tightly in their fists. Soon they were seated in the front row, from where they had a good view of the ring in which the dogs would be shown.

Rodney looked at his ticket and said to Betsy, "My ticket is number nine."

"That's right," said Betsy. "I didn't know you knew how to read numbers already."

"Yes," Rodney replied, "I learned to read

numbers on TV. Let me see your ticket, and I'll read your number."

Betsy showed Rodney her ticket, and he said, "Yours is twelve."

"That's right," said Betsy, and she tucked her ticket into her coat pocket. "Now put your ticket away," she said to Rodney.

Rodney put the ticket into the pocket of his shirt, but in a moment he decided to put it into his pants pocket. A few minutes later he took it out again and put it into a pocket on the right side of his jacket. Before long Rodney decided to put the ticket into the pocket on the left side of his jacket. Soon he had another idea. He put it in the back pocket of his trousers. Then the thought came to him that somebody might steal it out of his back pocket, so he took it out again and sat with it in his hands. After a few minutes he stuck the ticket into the side of his right shoe. At last he felt that the ticket was safe.

In a few moments the dogs were led in on leashes, each one by its owner. Toby was brought in by Jackie's father. The teacher called out, "Heel!" All of the dogs obeyed. Then she said, "Remove the leashes!" Now the dogs were free. The teacher said, "Sit!" All of the dogs sat.

When Betsy saw Toby obey the order, she thought, Why Toby is very obedient. He'll be sure to graduate.

At that moment Toby looked at the great Dane and barked. The great Dane looked at Toby and growled. Toby jumped up, and the great Dane jumped up. Then all the dogs jumped up. To everyone's surprise, Toby made for the door, which was open. The great Dane followed Toby. In a flash all the other dogs followed the great Dane.

Betsy and the children and many others left their seats and went to the door. They saw the dogs running up the street, followed by their owners, each one with a leash in his hand. The dogs were barking, and their owners were calling out, "Mike, come back!" "Toby, come back!" "Beauty, come back!" "Pete, come back!" Not one dog came back. They just kept on running after the great Dane and Toby, until finally they were caught and brought back by their owners.

When they were back in the ring, the teacher said, "That Toby! I don't think Toby has learned anything. He can't graduate."

Betsy heard Jackie crying behind her. The noise she was making was as bad as any bark from Toby. "Oh, oh, oh!" Jackie cried. "Toby can't graduate." Betsy turned around and saw that Jackie had her head in her mother's lap and was kicking the chair with her feet. She was screaming, "I want Toby to graduate!"

Betsy got up and went back and knelt down beside Jackie and her mother. "Don't cry,

Jackie," she said. "Toby will graduate some-day."

"I want him to graduate now!" Jackie said, sobbing.

Finally her mother quieted her, and most of the dogs behaved better. They seemed ashamed for having run away and wanted to make up for their bad behavior.

Betsy thought Rodney didn't show much interest in the dogs. All he cared about was getting that puppy for his own.

Finally a voice came over the loudspeaker. "We shall now have the drawing of the ticket for the door prize."

Rodney felt in his pants pocket for his ticket. It wasn't there! He felt in his shirt pocket. No ticket!

Betsy felt Rodney squirming around. "Rodney, what's the matter?" she asked.

"I can't find my ticket!" Rodney replied.

"You don't need it right now," Betsy said, as she watched a man put his hand into a large bowl and pull out a ticket.

The man put on his glasses and read the ticket. Then he called out, "The winner is number nineteen. Will the person who has ticket number nineteen bring it to me and receive the puppy?"

Rodney had been holding his breath. Now he let it out, and it sounded like the air coming out of a balloon. Betsy put her hand over Rodney's and said, "I'm sorry, Rodney." Rodney, with tears in his eyes, looked around to see who had the ticket that was number nineteen.

A little girl was making her way to the front of the room. She had her ticket in her hand, and her face was shining. When she reached the man, Rodney saw her hand the ticket to the man. The man looked at it. Then he said, "Oh, I'm sorry, but you were looking at this ticket upside down. This is sixty-one, not nineteen. Too bad!

Now where is nineteen? Will nineteen please come forward?"

No one came forward. Then a woman's voice from the back of the room called out, "My friend had number nineteen, but she's gone home. She has three poodles, and she doesn't want another one."

The little girl who had made the mistake looked very sad as she went back to her seat.

Rodney was still looking for his ticket as the man reached into the bowl the second time. In a moment he called out, "The winner is number nine. Will the person who has ticket number nine bring it to me and receive the puppy?"

"It's here," Betsy called out. "Number nine is right here." Then she said to Rodney, "You won the puppy after all. Isn't that wonderful! Now take your ticket to the man, and he'll give you the puppy."

Rodney's face was as red as a flag. He was

pulling all his pockets inside out. "Oh, Betsy," he cried, "I can't find it! I can't find it."

Meanwhile, the man was calling out, "Will number nine please come forward? If number nine doesn't have the ticket, we shall draw again."

Betsy stood up. "Oh, please!" she said. "Please wait. The little boy is looking for his ticket. I'm sure he'll find it."

Tears were running down Rodney's face. "Betsy, Betsy!" he was crying. "What shall I do?" Rodney began to crawl on the floor, looking for his ticket.

Just then a man behind Rodney said, "Look, Sonny, isn't that your ticket, sticking out of the side of your shoe?"

Rodney looked. He pulled the ticket out and stood up. His tears dried on his cheeks, and with a big smile he cried, "I found it! I found it!" Then he climbed over everyone in his way to the man holding the puppy, and the man put the puppy into Rodney's arms. As Rodney came back to Betsy she thought she had never seen a happier face.

Betsy was able to buy a leash for the puppy right there at the school, and she and the children started for home. All the children wanted to walk with Rodney and the puppy. They kept stooping down to pet the puppy. Rodney took only a few steps at a time, because the puppy had to lie down every few minutes to rest. Finally Rodney picked it up and carried it the rest of the way.

When they reached Rodney's house, Betsy said, "What are you going to name your puppy?"

"Oh, Tinkie," Rodney replied. "He's Tinkie for sure."

# Chapter 10

## THE LAST DAY

BETSY had enjoyed having the children in her play school. The five weeks had been full of fun, and she could hardly believe that they were nearly over. The time had almost come for Betsy and Star to visit their grandparents. Betsy had saved the money she had earned, and she had liked seeing her savings grow in the bank. Now she could buy a present for her grandparents.

Friday would be the last day, and Betsy wanted to make it a special day. She had decided to let the children dress up in some costumes that were in a big box in the attic, but she would keep her plan a secret from the children until Friday.

On Thursday morning Rodney rushed into the room, all out of breath, and said, "Can I bring my friend to school tomorrow?"

"Of course," said Betsy. "Do you have a new friend?"

"Another make-believe!" said Jackie.

Fay leaned over to Nancy and whispered, "Rodney has another make-believe friend."

Nancy giggled. "He's silly," she said. "Always having make-believe friends."

Rodney heard what Fay said, and he shouted, "He's not make-believe! He's real as real!"

Then he said to Betsy, "He's big! He's six, but he plays with me. His name is Cap."

"Where does Cap live?" Betsy asked.

"He just moved into a house across the street from us," Rodney replied.

"How nice for you," said Betsy.

"Does he have a make-believe dog?" Sammy asked.

"No, he has a real dog," replied Rodney, "like my real dog." Looking up at Betsy, he added, "And do you know what?"

"What?" said Betsy.

"My dog scared Bobo's dog away. Bobo's dog is all gone," Rodney replied. "And I'll tell you something else. Cap's grandfather lives in the country, and he bought Cap a pony. A real live pony!"

"Does he keep the pony across the street from you, Rodney?" Sammy asked, grinning.

"No," Rodney replied, "he keeps it in his grandfather's barn. When he goes to see his grandfather, he rides the pony."

The following morning Rodney arrived with Cap. He was a roly-poly little boy with bright red hair and a nose covered with freckles. Everything made him giggle.

Betsy wondered about the name of Rodney's new friend, so she said, "Why do they call you Cap?"

"You see," said Cap, "I have two grandfathers."

A chorus came from the other children, "So have I! So have I!"

"Like I said," Cap continued, "I have two grandfathers. Now my grandfather who bought me the pony, his name is Grandfather Elliot, but my other grandfather, he's Captain Oliver

Henry. He was captain of a great big ship. Well, I got named after him, so everybody used to call me Little Cap. Now I'm just Cap."

"Is your real name Oliver Henry?" asked Betsy.

"That's right," the boy replied, "but I like Cap better. I like boats, and I have a boat that I'm captain of."

"Oh, boy!" said Sammy. "He has a boat!"

"How nice that you have a boat," said Betsy. "Where do you sail your boat?"

"In the bathtub," Cap replied.

"Oh," said Betsy. "I guess I can't go sailing with you then."

Rodney spoke up. "Bobo has a sailboat, a great big sailboat."

Cap looked up at Betsy and said, "I never knew a kid before who had a make-believe friend. Bobo's are just for little kids, and I told Rodney so. I'm his real friend now." Then Cap turned to Rodney and said, "Didn't I tell you?"

Rodney's cheeks grew pink, and he said, "I forgot."

Cap looked around the room and said to Betsy, "What do you do here?"

"We do all kinds of things," Betsy replied.

"Rodney says you eat cookies and drink milk," said Cap.

"After a while we'll have some cookies and drink milk," said Betsy, "but today is our last day, and we're going to do something special."

"Like what?" Cap asked.

"You'll see," said Betsy.

"Is it a secret?" Rosie asked.

"Yes, it's a secret," Betsy replied.

"Tell us! Tell us!" Jackie and Fay called out together.

"You'll find out very soon," said Betsy.

A short time later Betsy called upstairs to her mother.

Her mother came to the head of the stairs. "Yes, Betsy, what do you want?"

Betsy replied, "I think we're ready for that big box in the attic that I spoke to you about. Do you think you could get it down now?"

"Oh," cried Fay, "there's something in a box!"

"Sure," Cap called out. "There's always a Jack-in-the-box!"

"I bet there's something better than that," said Nancy.

The little girls began to jump up and down, they were so excited.

Betsy's mother answered, "I'll get it down. It won't take me long."

"I'll come help you," said Betsy.

"Me too," said Rodney.

"I can do it without any help," said her mother.

"Oh, dear," said Rodney. "I wanted to see the attic."

"Well, I'll come just in case," said Betsy.

Betsy started up the basement stairs, and the seven children followed. By the time they climbed the stairs to the second floor, Betsy's mother was already in the attic.

"You children just wait down there," she said.

The children looked up at the open trapdoor. They thought that the large piece cut out of the ceiling and the ladderlike steps extending from the opening to the floor looked strange. "Can I come up?" Rodney asked.

"No!" replied Betsy's mother. "No one can come up. I'm bringing the box down in a minute."

"Can I sit on the steps?" Rodney asked Betsy.

"Of course you can sit on the steps until Mother comes down," said Betsy.

Rodney and Sammy sat down on the steps of the ladder. The rest of the children stood looking up, watching for Betsy's mother to appear.

In a moment they saw her. She was carrying a big box. Just as she reached the top of the steps, she dropped the box. The lid flew off, and the box and all of the clothes came flying down through the opening above. Trousers, skirts, hats, false faces, shawls—left over from all sorts of Halloween costumes—fell on the children, while the box and the lid fell with a bang on the floor.

"Oh, Mother!" Betsy cried out.

"Oh, dear," cried Betsy's mother, looking down at the children, who now were trying to get out from under the clothes. "I hope I didn't hurt anyone."

Rodney had a clown's false face sitting on the top of his head and a pair of trousers hanging around his shoulders. Rosie was covered with a

black-lace shawl and looked as if she had been caught in a net. Sammy's head was completely covered by a high silk hat. Fay was on the floor, trying to crawl out from under a white bunny-rabbit suit. When she emerged, she held it up and said, "Oh, I'm going to be the Easter bunny!"

"Not the Easter bunny," said Nancy. "Peter Rabbit!"

Jackie picked up a bright red skirt. "I'm going to be Little Red Riding Hood," she said.

"That isn't a hood," said Nancy. "That's a skirt."

"When I put it on, it will be a hood," said Jackie.

The children gathered up the clothes, and when Betsy's mother came down from the attic, she put the clothes back into the box. Then the children watched her as she pushed the steps back up into the attic and closed the trapdoor.

Rodney looked up and said, "Now there isn't any hole in the ceiling!"

"Just a door," said Sammy. "But it's a funny place to have a door—in the ceiling."

The children trooped down the stairs and back into the schoolroom. Betsy's mother placed the box on the table.

Betsy lifted the clothes out of the box and said, "Now you children can dress up in these things." Betsy pulled out one costume after the other as well as false faces, hats, and wigs.

She held up a fuzzy brown suit and said, "I wore this when I was in the first grade and I was an elf." She handed the suit to Cap. "Here, Cap, this will fit you. You can be an elf or one of the Seven Little Dwarfs."

Cap took the suit. "I don't want to be an elf or one of the Seven Little Dwarfs. I want to be a pony."

"Very well," said Betsy. "You can be a pony if you wish."

The children set to work putting on the costumes. There was a great deal of laughing and calling out, "Oh, look at him!" and "Oh, look at her!"

Fay climbed into the rabbit suit and said, "Now I'm the Easter bunny."

"That's just because you want to be the Easter bunny," said Jackie. "But you don't have any Easter basket or any Easter eggs. If you were the Easter bunny, you would have Easter eggs." Jackie began to sing out, "You're not the Easter bunny! You're not the Easter bunny!"

Betsy interrupted. "I think I have a basket," she said. "It's up in the toy closet. I'll get it." Betsy left the children and ran upstairs. When she came back, she was carrying a little basket. "Now just look!" she said. "This is a real Easter basket. I found two hard-boiled eggs in Mother's refrigerator. She said I could have them."

Fay took the basket and said, "Now I'm really the Easter bunny! I have an Easter basket and Easter eggs."

Jackie looked into the basket. "They aren't Easter eggs. They're just chicken eggs. Easter eggs are bright colors."

Fay looked sad but only for a moment. Then she said, "I can color them." She opened up two jars of paint and set to work painting the eggs. When she finished, she had a red egg and a green egg in the basket. "Now I'm the Easter bunny!" she called out to the children. "I'm going to hide the Easter basket outdoors, and you can all come out and look for it. But don't come until I say, 'Come!'"

Fay ran outside. She hid the basket behind a bush. Then she called, "Come!"

All the children came out into the yard dressed

in their costumes. Jackie had put the red skirt over her head like a hood, and Betsy had pinned it with a safety pin under her chin. The rest of the skirt hung down and covered her. Rodney was in a soldier suit, and Sammy was dressed like a pirate. Rosie was wearing a blue cape and a high pointed hat. As she came out the door she said to Betsy, "I'm Mother Goose!"

"It certainly looks like Halloween," said Betsy.

"Halloween in July!" Cap cried. "This is fun!"

Sammy laughed. "I never hunted for an Easter basket on Halloween before," he cried out.

The children scattered to look for the basket. "I hope I find the basket," said Jackie, "'cause I'm Red Riding Hood and I have to have a basket to carry goodies to my grandmother."

Suddenly Thumpy, who was in the yard, began to bark. "Now what is the matter with Thumpy?" said Betsy.

Star, who had just come outside, went to see what Thumpy was barking at. "Oh!" she cried. "Thumpy has found the Easter basket."

All the children came running to Star. Rodney was the first to reach her. He stooped down and looked into the basket. "Oh, there's a frog in the basket!" he shouted. "A frog is sitting on the Easter eggs." All the children leaned over to look at the frog.

Rodney picked up the basket and held it out to Jackie. "Here, Red Riding Hood," he said. "Here's a basket of goodies to take to your grandmother."

Jackie screamed and ran away, crying, "Oh, oh! Take it away! Take it away! I hate frogs!"

Rodney carried the basket to the little pool in the yard and said, "I'll dump the frog into the pool. He probably was in the pool and hopped out."

"Be careful of my Easter eggs," Fay cried out.

Rodney was not very careful, for as he dumped the frog into the pool the eggs fell out too.

"Oh, dear!" exclaimed Fay. "Now it isn't an Easter basket anymore."

Betsy came to the pool with a rake. "I'll fish the eggs out," she said.

The children squatted down around the pool and watched while Betsy caught hold of the eggs and lifted them out.

"Oh," cried Jackie, "they're just chicken eggs again! All the paint has washed off."

"Well, nobody wants Easter eggs that a frog has been sitting on," said Rodney.

Fay reached out for the eggs and said, "I'll peel the shells off and give the eggs to Thumpy, because he really found the Easter basket."

The children went back into the schoolroom and took off their fancy clothes. Everything was put back into the big box.

Then it was time for milk and cookies, and the children sat down at the table. Cap sat beside Rodney.

Betsy placed a cookie on the table for Rodney and one for Cap. Then she gave them each a carton of milk. Rodney reached out and said, "You didn't put a cookie down for Bobo, and where is Bobo's milk?"

"That guy Bobo again," Cap shouted. "I'm sitting on Bobo, Rodney. He's all squashed. I'm here. Pinch me if you want to, 'cause I'm real. You couldn't pinch Bobo."

"You scared him away," said Rodney.

Soon the time came for the children to go home. They gathered around Betsy. "Oh, we did have fun," said Jackie.

"You bet!" said Sammy. Then he tapped Cap

on the shoulder and said, "You know what, Bobo?"

Cap wheeled around and cried, "Don't you call me Bobo. My name's Cap, and I'm real, I am." All the children laughed. Rosie, laughing, called out, "Rodney brought a make-believe friend to play school, and now he's going home with a real friend."

Rodney said, "I'm glad I have a real friend. He's better than Bobo."

"Yippie," Cap cried, "I'm glad I'm real."

Fay looked up at Betsy. "Will kindergarten be as nice as play school? It's been such fun."

"Oh, it will be nicer," Betsy replied.

"Bet there won't be any jelly-bean mice to grow up and take on a picnic," said Sammy. "That was fun."

"Mice on a picnic!" Cap exclaimed. "What are jelly-bean mice?"

Before anyone could tell Cap about the mice,

Nancy said, "We had a Fourth of July picnic too."

Fay giggled. "Remember Rodney got his head stuck in a bucket, and Mr. Kilpatrick had to come and get it off!"

"Oh, yes," cried Sammy, "and we lost all the hot dogs!"

"Tell me more. Tell me more," said Cap. "You must have had a great time here."

"I'll tell you all about it going home," said Rodney.

"Can we come back next summer?" Fay asked Betsy.

"You can all come back," Betsy replied, feeling a bit sad as she waved good-bye to the children.

As Betsy straightened up the room, she found that she felt lonely without the children. Star and Lillybell were playing in the yard. Betsy called them in to help her put the chairs in order.

"It was a lot of fun, wasn't it, Betsy?" Star said.

"I think so," Betsy replied. "I hope it got them ready for kindergarten."

"Well, they can't take any make-believe kids with them," said Lillybell. "They know that's silly business."

Betsy and Star laughed.

"And no make-believe dogs," said Star.

Betsy laughed, and she found she didn't feel sad anymore.

## About the Author

Carolyn Haywood was born in Philadelphia and now lives in Chestnut Hill, a suburb of that city. A graduate of the Philadelphia Normal School, she also studied at the Pennsylvania Academy of Fine Arts, where she won the Cresson European Scholarship. Her first story, *"B" Is for Betsy,* was published in 1939. Since then she has written books almost every year and has become one of the most widely read American writers for younger children. In 1969, she was made a Distinguished Daughter of Pennsylvania.